The Barefoot Book of
Father
&
Daughter
TALES

For John and Rachel, and now for Benedict and Leah
— Josephine Evetts-Secker
For my father — Helen Cann

Barefoot Books
2067 Massachusetts Ave
Cambridge, MA 02140

Story CD narrated by Allan Corduner
Recording and CD production by Sans Walk Spoken Word Studio, England

First published in the United States of America by Barefoot Books, Inc in 1997
This edition first published in 2012

Graphic design by Judy Linard, London
Color separation by Grafiscan, Verona
Printed in China on 100% acid-free paper
This book was typeset in Perpetua 13 on 21 point, Trajan, Centaur and Raniscript
The illustrations were prepared in watercolor

ISBN 978-1-84686-761-3

Library of Congress Cataloging-in-Publication Data is available under
LCCN 2011048295

1 3 5 7 9 8 6 4 2

The Barefoot Book of

Father
&
Daughter
TALES

RETOLD BY *Josephine Evetts~Secker*

ILLUSTRATED BY *Helen Cann*

NARRATED BY *Allan Corduner*

Barefoot Books
step inside a story

CONTENTS

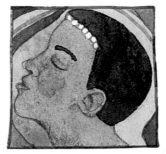

FOREWORD

M ost folk and fairy tales have at their center some aspect of the family drama. This anthology concentrates on the drama enacted between father and daughter. How can a father love his daughter wisely and well? This has always been, and remains, a dilemma. The bond between a father and his daughter is full of dangers as well as delights. And both sides struggle with the tension in being too close, or not close enough.

In this book there are stories about the daughters of gods and woodcutters, kings and poor farmers, viziers, rich merchants and warriors. How the father treats his daughter and his attitude to her is usually what sparks the drama. Then often the father disappears from the story until the end, when there is a reconciliation, or a resolution to complete the adventure and begin a new way of life. A new relationship is created between father and daughter, which is appropriate for a young adult woman and expresses mutual respect.

Folk and fairy tales are full of fathers who love, yet fail, either through weakness or inflexibility. But their mistakes become the windows through which new and unexpected possibilities appear.

Fairy tales do not always end in perfection. They work towards repair and wholeness in a world that will always be imperfect. Fairy tales tell us that failure is just part of being human, but as long as the heart is generous, we can learn from our mistakes and move on. The only failing that is not tolerated in fairy tales is evil itself: meanness of spirit and the refusal to be generous.

In most cultures, fathers traditionally embody authority, yet in fairy tales they are particularly likely to fail. They may work hard to achieve their own high-minded goals, but often the truth lies elsewhere and they are fooling themselves and chasing after the wrong ideals. Fairy tales ask us always to remember this. We might think that the fathers who control their daughters' lives are worthy and wise, but more often than not, they are foolish and need to learn from their daughters. Fathers must sometimes be defied, and daughters must often question their authority. The daughters in these stories must plead again and again for what they feel in their hearts — and so often it is this that turns out to be necessary at the end of the story.

Daughters have to free themselves from the too-loving father as well as from the tyrannical father, and this freedom is often symbolized through marriage. With this sacred ritual, the daughter lets go of her father and unites with an "other."

In the stories you are about to read, you will watch fathers struggling to love warmly and properly, and also to be loved by their daughters. They have to try to teach their daughters to behave in the right way in the worlds they inhabit, and yet stay true to themselves. They will struggle to protect their daughters as much as they can, to guide them while letting them make their own decisions and encouraging them whenever they can. These are the responsibilities and gifts that good fathers offer their daughters.

It is not surprising that these stories are full of contradictions and questions. There is no simple rule book; all fathers and all daughters must find their own way. And that is part of the excitement and fascination of these tales. As the Dinka story begins, "Listen to this ancient tale!" The authority of this voice has held us in its power for centuries and still has energy to do so.

Josephine Evetts-Secker
Whitby, 2011

THE FROG PRINCE

GERMAN

Long, long ago, when wishing still worked, there lived a king with several daughters, the youngest of whom was so fair that she seemed brighter than the sun.

Around the king's castle grew a great forest. In the midst of the forest stood an ancient lime tree, and beneath this tree was a very deep well. When the days were warm, the youngest princess would go out alone into the forest and sit dreamily beside the well. Then she would rouse herself and play with her golden ball, throwing it into the air and catching it as it fell, gleaming in the sunlight. She loved this ball best of all her possessions. One summer day, when she was playing beside the well, the princess threw her golden ball too high and when it fell back down through the air it missed her open hands and dropped into the cold waters of the well. Though the princess peered long into its depths, she

8

could not see it at all. She began to cry, and then to weep helplessly, fearing that her ball was lost forever.

In the midst of her tears, she heard a curious voice speaking to her. "Fair daughter of the king, why do you cry?" it asked. "Your weeping will make even the hard stones feel pity."

She looked around in bewilderment, for she saw no one nearby. Then her eye caught sight of a slimy green frog sitting by the side of the well, gazing straight at her from its round, black eyes. "Oh, it's you, old pond-hopper," she exclaimed. "Well, if you must know, I am crying for my golden ball, which has fallen down into the dark well."

"I can help you," the frog informed her, "but you must offer me something in return. What will it be?"

"If you can bring back my golden ball to me," the princess quickly replied, "I will give you anything you desire, my jewels, my gowns, even my crown!"

"I have no desire for your wealth, nor even for your golden crown. What I desire is your heart," the frog began. "I would be the happiest of creatures if you would be my friend and let me play with you and one day come to love me. I would sit beside you at the table and eat from your golden plate, and I would sleep with you in your soft bed to keep you company. For this I will rescue your golden ball."

"What nonsense, how can I possibly be friends with a frog?" the princess thought to herself. But she said aloud, "Yes, of course, you can certainly have what you wish, only please fetch me my golden ball at once."

"Do you promise to be my friend?" the frog asked, as he prepared to hop into the well.

Without a second thought, the princess said, "Most certainly I promise," impatiently stamping her foot.

Instantly, the frog dived beneath the dark waters and came back up after a few minutes with the golden ball. He threw it on the grass and the princess grabbed it at once and ran merrily back to the castle.

"Wait! Wait for me," the frog gasped, as he tried to hop after her. But she was gone, without so much as a backwards glance. Sobbing quietly, the green frog slid back into the water.

The next day, the princess had forgotten all about the loss of her golden ball and the help of the green frog and she played in the castle till dinner time. Then, as she sat with her father at the table and began to eat from her golden plate and drink from her golden cup, she heard a slithery sound coming slowly up the marble stairs. A voice she recognized croaked from the door, "Princess, daughter of the king, please open the door for me." She ignored the cry and with a pounding heart went on eating. But the cries became more and more insistent and the king saw that she was afraid.

"Dear child, what is the matter?" he asked. "Anyone would think there was a giant outside waiting to pounce on you."

"It's not a giant, papa, but a horrible, slimy frog," she explained.

"A frog? What does a frog want here?"

"Father, I am so afraid," she cried. "A frog rescued my golden ball when it fell down the well yesterday. Because I wanted it back, I promised him anything he liked if he fetched it for me. And now he wants to claim what I promised him," she wept, "and he is so ugly. Please send him away."

But the frog went on banging at the door and croaking:

Fairest princess with the golden ball,

Open the door when I come to call.

You promised me love,

You promised me play,

And here I come to claim them today.

He sang this song over and over again, while the king grew very serious and said, "My dear daughter, you must always keep your promise. He gave you what you desired, and now it is your turn to grant his wish. Go and open the door and let the frog come in." Reluctantly the princess opened the door and she was followed back to her chair by the slithery frog.

"Pick me up, pick me up," he called out, "for I can't reach the table on my own." So the princess had to lift him up to the table, where he sat beside her and ate from her golden plate. She could scarcely swallow her food, but he ate with great delight, till he could eat no more. When they had both finished, he said, "I am very tired now. Please take me with you to bed."

The princess could not bear to think of the frog lying on her white satin sheets, but the king said severely, "You must not despise the one who helped you." So most unwillingly she carried the frog up to her room. She couldn't bear to let him be close to her, for he seemed so cold and slimy. So she put him in a corner and lay down alone between her snowy sheets.

Up hopped the frog beside her with the words, "I am so tired. Please let me rest beside you, for you promised me your heart and your friendship."

Hearing this and feeling him near, the king's daughter was so angry and afraid that she picked up the frog and hurled it against the wall, shouting, "You disgusting little creature. Go away!"

Then, to her astonishment, the bruised frog turned into a young man, who stood looking at her with beautiful dark eyes.

"I am a king's son," he explained quietly, "and I claim you as my bride. Your father has already urged you to keep the promises you made to me." Then he told her how an evil witch had changed him into the form of a frog, in which he was fated to remain until a princess would let him sleep upon her bed.

The next morning, a coach arrived to take the young couple back to the prince's kingdom. The king was delighted that his daughter had honored her promise and that she had found her bridegroom with whom she might reign in peace.

ALUEL AND HER
LOVING FATHER

DINKA (SUDAN)

Listen to this ancient tale!
Ayak was beautiful. She was wooed by Chol, a herdsman, and gave
birth to a daughter as beautiful as herself. Soon after, Ayak died. Her husband,
Chol, was in despair but he took the newborn baby and rocked her on his lap,
while the people of his village said, "You can't do that. Find another woman to
mother her."

Chol refused, saying, "No, I will hold my own child and care for her." So
he kept his daughter with him in the cow barn, and he called her Aluel. He
fed her on milk till she grew into a young girl. He alone took care of her and
taught her to speak.

One day as they sat together, Aluel said to him, "Father, why do you stay alone without another wife? Will I never have brothers and sisters?"

"Little Aluel," he replied, "I do not marry again because I fear that a stepmother might not love you, or might make me forget you. So I stay alone and care only for you."

"It is not right to stay alone," Aluel said, and she continued to pester him with such talk for months. Eventually, he relented and married again. "This is my child, Aluel," he told his new wife, "and for her sake, I did not want to marry, so that I could love only her and remember my first wife through her. But my little girl has spoken wise words, and I have agreed to find another wife. So you must take care of her, or you cannot live with me."

At first, the stepmother treated Aluel kindly, but soon she began to starve her. Chol asked, "Little Aluel, why is your belly like that? Are you not eating?" But Aluel did not want to make her father unhappy. She kept the truth to herself and always said, "Yes, of course I am eating, but I am not hungry now."

Then another daughter was born, and she was fed well by her mother, while Aluel became thinner and thinner. When this daughter was old enough to speak, she asked her mother, "Why do you treat my stepsister so unkindly? She is hungry and you do not feed her."

Her mother was angry and asked, "How can you say such a thing? And now I suppose you will go and tell your father about me and he will not care for me anymore. I forbid you to say any more." So her daughter did not tell her father or anyone else, and life became harder and harder for Aluel.

Then one day, Aluel reproached her father, "Why have you never been to visit my mother's family? You do not even go to see how my grandmother is

and to tell her I am well. You do not even go to collect the cattle, my mother's bridewealth. We need some more cattle now."

And her father replied, "It is because I fear to leave you that I never go far from this village. I am afraid that you will be harmed." Aluel laughed at his fear and again he thought he should do as his daughter suggested.

While he was away, Aluel missed him sorely. Her stepmother took advantage of Chol's absence and played a cruel trick. As the sun was setting, she told Aluel that she could see a man standing near the sun, and that it must be Chol. "Go and run to him and greet him," she encouraged the girl.

Off Aluel ran, nearer and nearer to the sun, looking for her father. She ran further and further and never returned, for when she reached the big river, she fell in and was rescued by the sun.

"Where have you come from?" the sun asked, and Aluel explained how she had been sent off by her stepmother. The sun was very sad to hear that she had no mother to love her, so he took her home. The sun told her he had two wives who had no children of their own, and that they would take good care of her. The wives were happy to have a child to look after and they grew to love Aluel very much.

Meanwhile, Chol returned home and found that his little Aluel had disappeared. He was immediately afraid for her and raved in his despair. He refused all comfort and grew wilder and wilder, so that soon he had to be chained in his cow barn. There he sat, shouting all day and night.

Each morning as the sun rose, and each evening when he fell, he passed by the barn of Chol and saw his misery. Eventually, he told his wives that they must let Aluel go back to her father, for he was suffering unbearably. The wives resisted his decision, but the sun had made up his mind.

When the sun next passed by Chol's village, he called out, "Man in the cow barn! Listen to me. I am the sun, and I have seen your misery, day after day, as I passed over your barn. I have comfort for you. Little Aluel is not dead. She is living with two sun mothers who take good care of her. But I will bring her back to you."

Chol began to cry when he heard that his Aluel was safe, and he begged to know what had happened to her. The sun said, "I am late, I must hurry, so listen carefully. You must cut some poles and make a high platform with them. I will bring Aluel to you there in a few days and will place her on the platform."

Chol called to the people of his village and asked for milk. Then he asked for food. Then he asked to be released from his chains. When the villagers saw that he was no longer raving, all this was done for him. Then he went into the forest to cut the trees to make the platform. After three days, the sun brought Aluel back to her father and Chol secretly took her down from the platform and hid her in his barn.

On that same day, a young man named Ring had a vision, in which he saw Aluel brought to her father's barn by the sun. Ring had never met a girl who touched his heart. But when he saw Aluel in his vision, he said to his father, "I have seen the girl I want to marry, and I must travel a long way to find her."

Then Ring asked his father to release cows to take as a dowry, and he set off, accompanied by other young men from his village. When they arrived at Chol's village, Ring announced that he had come to marry Chol's daughter. The stepmother was delighted and prepared her own daughter to be the bride. Chol sat in front of his cow barn where Aluel was still hidden, and he entertained

Ring and his friends. A bull was killed and roasted, but Ring would not eat.

"We will not begin to feast," he announced, "until the bride herself comes out to serve us water."

Chol was surprised at this and answered, "But my daughter has already served you. She is the bride."

"No, no. I desire your other daughter," Ring persisted. "The daughter who followed the sun. She has been brought back by the sun and you are hiding her in your barn."

"How do you know these things?" asked the puzzled father.

"I have seen these things in a vision," answered Ring. "I know where she is."

And so Chol called Aluel out of the barn and everyone was amazed to see her. Aluel took water to Ring and his friends and the marriage was celebrated.

19

THE GREEN KNIGHT

DANISH

Once upon a time, a princess was born to a king and queen. But soon after her birth, the queen fell ill. Knowing that she would soon die, she called her husband to her and made him promise that he would give their daughter anything she ever begged from him. With that she died peacefully.

The king grieved at his wife's death and felt that his heart would break. But he took comfort in his child. She was sad and gentle and liked to wander alone through gardens and woods, speaking to the animals and picking flowers.

One morning, while she was wandering through the woods, she came across a poor widow and her daughter gathering firewood. The widow was a sly woman, and the daughter vain and selfish. The young girl stopped to talk to them, and when the widow and her daughter discovered that she was a princess, they plotted to make the princess enjoy their company. From then

20

on, the widow and her daughter met the princess whenever she visited the woods, and always spoke kindly to her. After a few weeks, the princess enjoyed their company so much that she looked forward to these meetings.

One day, the widow told her that they had hardly any money, and they were going to seek work in a distant town. The princess was unhappy to lose her new friends and begged them to come and live in the palace. The widow pretended to think hard and then exclaimed, "Why, I am alone with a daughter, and your father, too, is alone with a daughter. Perhaps we could live happily together and take care of each other?"

The princess was delighted and ran home to her father, begging him to marry the widow so that the two girls could stay together. "She is the only friend I have," the princess implored, "and the widow treats me kindly, just like a mother." The king could not resist her pleas and agreed to marry, against his better judgement. There was a fine wedding and they lived in the palace together. At first, all went well. But after a few months the stepmother began to mistreat the princess and to favor her own daughter.

The king was distressed when he saw what was happening. "Alas, my child," he grieved, "I cannot bear to see you so ill-used. I should have denied you your wish. But now it is too late and the widow is my wife." He decided to send his daughter away so that she would be spared the stepmother's cruelty. "You must take two ladies-in-waiting with you to my summer palace on the island in the lake. There you will be safe and I will visit you often," he promised.

The princess was sorrowful at the prospect of being parted from her beloved father, but there was no other way to escape the wicked woman and her envious daughter.

So she went to live with her ladies-in-waiting on the island. It was a lonely life, though she was happy enough walking in the gardens and listening to the birdsong. In this way, she spent her days and grew into a most beautiful young woman. But her heart was often filled with a strange longing; for what she could not tell — perhaps a knight as green as grass.

One day, her father was sadder than usual when he visited her. "My dear, I must go away on a journey and I may not see you for a long time." He sighed as he kissed her good-bye.

The princess sighed too and said as they parted, "Father, if on your travels you meet a green knight, tell him that I greet him, and that I long for him to come to me, for he alone can help overcome my sadness."

"I will grant you your desire," her father promised, as he rowed away.

The king was gone for many months and though he met many knights and many kings, he heard no mention of the Green Knight and felt very sorry that he could not fulfill his daughter's request. Eventually, he began his homeward journey, crossing mountains and streams, till he came to a deep, dark forest. He made his way through the crowded trees until he came suddenly into a clearing full of wild boars. A young herdsman sat in their midst, playing a pipe that quietened the wild animals, so that they fed peacefully.

"Whose animals are these, and whose herdsman are you?" the king asked.

"These beasts belong to the Green Knight who lives far east of here," replied the herdsman, and returned to his pipe.

The king was delighted to hear about the Green Knight and hastened eastward for three days, till he reached a pasture filled with elk and wild oxen, also grazing quietly to the sounds of a herdsman's pipe.

"Whose animals are these?" the king asked, "and who is your master?"

"I serve the Green Knight and to him these beasts belong," the herdsman answered.

"I must go to your master," the king said, hoping to find the knight his daughter desired. "Please tell me where he lives that I might visit him."

When he heard that he must travel another day eastward, the king eagerly set off again, and in time came through green forests and fields to a great castle, covered with green ivy. When he rode up to the castle, the Green Knight came out to meet him.

"I have traveled far to find you," the king said, "for my daughter requests that I greet you in her name."

The knight responded without surprise to the message, saying, "It is not for me that your daughter waits. She is sad and seeks rest and was thinking of death in the green earth when she gave you her message. But I will send her a gift that may comfort her."

Then he offered the king a green book, saying, "Tell your daughter that whenever she is unhappy she should open her east window and sit there to read this green book."

The king thanked the knight for his kindness and after spending the night as his guest, he set off for home. He went first to the island to see his daughter, to tell her what had happened and give her the green book.

That evening, the princess sat at her window, open to the east, and looked into the strange book sent by the Green Knight. It was written in a language unknown to her, and yet she began to understand the curious poems. She read the first verse aloud:

> *The wind is restless over the land,*
> *Blowing the earth and sea and sand.*
> *Will love be promised, true and deep,*
> *Before the world falls into sleep?*

As she spoke the words of the first verse, the wind blew past her and out to the lake; at the second verse, the wind shook the trees at the water's edge; at the third verse, her maids fell into a sudden sleep. Then a bird flew in through her window.

The bird at once assumed human form and spoke to her. "Do not be afraid," he said. "I am the Green Knight and I have come to listen to your sorrow."

The princess was overjoyed, and found herself talking to him freely, as though she had known him all her life.

"I will come to you in this way whenever you want me," the knight told her after they had talked for many hours. "When you are ready to rest, just close the book and I will immediately return to my castle as quietly as I came."

She closed the book and fell into a dream-filled sleep. Her dream was of the Green Knight and the happiness of the dream stayed with her day after day, so that she became bright and healthy and began to laugh and play with her ladies-in-waiting.

The king was delighted to see his daughter happy again and felt certain that she was healed by the wisdom of the green book. No one knew about her conversations with the Green Knight.

On his third visit, the knight gave the princess a golden ring and they were secretly betrothed. They had to wait three months, however, before he could ask the king for his daughter's hand in marriage.

Meanwhile, the stepmother grew very suspicious at the news of the girl's blossoming happiness, for she had hoped that when she was alone on the island she would pine away and die, so that her own child would receive the king's affection. So she sent spies to watch the girl; first her ladies-in-waiting and then her daughter. They all reported the same thing: that everyone fell asleep in the evening when the princess sat at her window. Eventually, the queen herself went to find out what was happening to make the girl so happy. She thought that someone must be coming in through the open window, so she put poisoned scissors on the ledge and kept watch. But she, too, fell asleep and did not see the bird fly in; nor did she hear the talk between the lovers.

"How happy I am that we must wait only one more week before you can go to ask my father for my hand in marriage," the princess exclaimed joyfully to the Green Knight.

"And then you will come with me to my green castle in the midst of my green forests and fields," he responded.

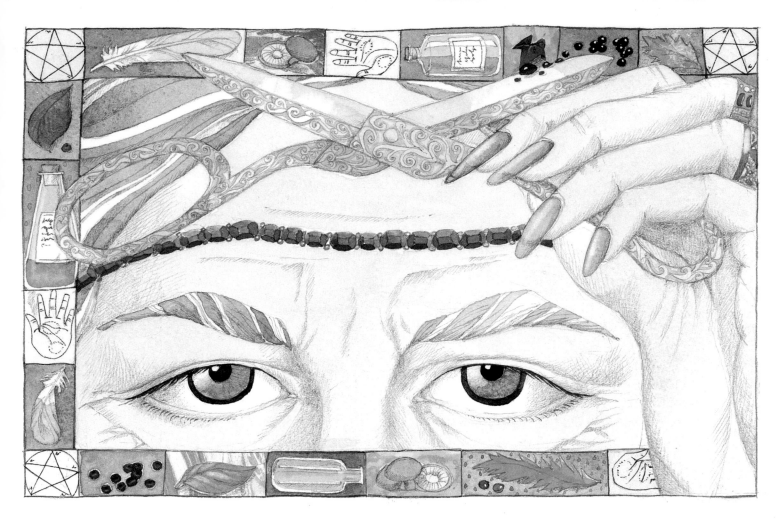

When the princess grew tired and closed the book, the knight resumed his bird shape to fly away, but he flew too low through the window and grazed a leg on the scissors. He escaped with a cry that woke the princess. From that moment, she became unhappy again.

The queen found her scissors and rejoiced that they were covered with blood. Satisfied that her plan had worked, she picked up the scissors and went back to her palace.

The princess was so weak by the next evening that she could scarcely open her book, and when she did so, no bird came, though the wind rushed over the lake and through the trees. In despair, she tried to summon her knight the next evening, and the next. But no bird came.

One day, as she wandered in her garden, she overheard two ravens talking about herself and the Green Knight. The first said, "How sad that the knight lies sick and only our princess can heal him. Yet she knows nothing of his wound from the queen's poisoned scissors."

The other raven asked, "How can the Green Knight be healed if the princess knows nothing of his fate?"

The first raven replied, "In the king's courtyard there is a nest of adders. If the princess can catch and cook these, and serve them to the knight, he will be cured. Otherwise, he will die."

As she listened to the conversation, the princess resolved to help the knight and made plans to travel to her father's palace.

As soon as night came, she took the boat and rowed across the lake by the light of the moon and stars. Quietly, she made her way to the courtyard, where she found nine adders and wrapped them in her apron. Then she set out to find the Green Knight's castle. It was a long journey and by the time she arrived her clothes were torn and dirty and no one would have believed she was a princess. She entered the castle just as the doctors were declaring that the knight had no hope of recovery.

The princess begged to work in the kitchen, where she prepared a soup made of three of the adders. When the knight drank it, his fever abated and he asked the cook for more. The next day, she made soup from another three adders, and the knight was able to sit up in bed. His courtiers were amazed. On the third day, the princess made the soup from the last three adders. When the knight drank it, he felt so much better that he ran down to the kitchen to thank the kitchen maid.

As soon as he entered the kitchen, he recognized his betrothed, and, indeed, she had put on his golden ring. So there could be no doubt.

The couple embraced and wept and decided to marry at once. They sent a message to the king to ask for his blessing and to invite him to share their joy. He was delighted that his daughter had found her Green Knight. He set off immediately to celebrate his daughter's wedding, and to live with her at the Green Knight's castle.

BEAUTY AND THE BEAST

FRENCH

Once upon a time, there was a merchant with three sons and three daughters. The youngest daughter was dearly loved by her father, for she was kind and witty. Because she was so beautiful, she was called "Beauty." As they grew up together, her sisters grew more and more envious of her and made fun of her at every opportunity, for they resented the fact that Beauty was sought out by the richest and handsomest young men, whom she always refused courteously. She said that she was not ready to leave her father.

One terrible day, the father's fleet was lost at sea with all its cargo, and the family fell into great poverty. They had to leave their home in the city and went to lead a simple life in the woods. Beauty quietly began to look after the house, caring for everyone as the servants had once done. Her father and brothers were most grateful for this, though her sisters scorned her.

30

Many months later, the father's fortunes began to turn again and he returned to the city to attend to his affairs. The older sisters clamored for him to bring them back new dresses, but Beauty said nothing till he asked, "And now, dear Beauty, what can I bring back for you? You have worked so hard and so kindly for us all. I must bring you a gift too." Beauty thought for a while and then said, "I would like you to bring back a single red rose."

Business did not go well for the merchant and he set off for home feeling discouraged. One night, he was caught in a terrible storm and he had to seek shelter in a castle that he could not remember seeing before in that place. "I am sure I will be safe here on such a night," he thought, as he entered the well-lit courtyard. He called out, but no one replied. He decided to enter the castle and went from room to room till he reached a dining hall, where a fine meal was set out on the table and a fire burned brightly in the grate. Again he called out, but still there was no reply. Since the place felt so warm and welcoming, he sat down to eat, expecting someone to appear at any moment. Once his hunger was satisfied, he felt so tired that he went to find a room in which to sleep. "It seems that I have been expected," he thought, as he lay down on a freshly made bed in a warm chamber.

When the merchant woke, clean clothes replaced the muddy ones of the day before, and breakfast was laid out for him as though he were a welcome guest. The sun now shone, and before he left the castle he wandered in the garden to enjoy its beauty. Suddenly his eyes fell on a beautiful red rose, gleaming as the dew melted in the morning sun. "I must take this home for my dearest Beauty," he decided, reaching out to pluck the rose. But as he did so, he heard a bellowing roar and a monstrous figure rose up before him.

"How dare you steal my rose!" screamed the beast. "How ungrateful you are for my hospitality! For such an offence you must pay with your life."

The frightened merchant fell on his knees and pleaded, "I am truly sorry that I have offended you. I did not think it theft to take such a small gift for my dearest daughter, who asked for a red rose when I parted from her."

"You should think more about what you are doing," the beast snarled. "You must be punished. However, if you go home and ask one of your daughters to come back in your place, then I will let you go free. Otherwise, say good-bye to your family and return to me within three months."

The merchant left the beast's castle and sadly made his way home, carrying the single red rose for Beauty. His children greeted him joyfully, but their happiness turned to grief when they heard his tale. Beauty did not hesitate for a moment, but insisted that she was ready to take her father's place and go to the beast. But the merchant would hear nothing of it. "No, no, you cannot suffer on my account," he insisted to Beauty. "Only let me enjoy your company for a little while, then we will say good-bye and I shall return to the castle."

But Beauty was determined to go in her father's place. "I cannot bear to live without you," she said, "so I will follow you there if you will not let me go alone. I have made up my mind."

Everyone wept as Beauty and her father prepared to leave, though the sons' grief was more genuine than the sisters'. Soon they came to the beast's castle. Food and fresh beds were ready as before and, to their amazement, they slept well and woke refreshed. Beauty had dreamed of an old fairy woman, who made her feel less afraid. After they had spoken of her dream, she told her father, "Now you must leave me to my fate. It must be so."

With a heavy heart, her father kissed her and departed. After she had waved him good-bye, she wandered through the marvelous gardens and great chambers of the castle. In one particularly lovely room she saw her own name on the door. There she sat and wept for her father. As she did so, she saw that the mirror before her showed her the scene of his safe arrival home, and she felt much happier.

At midday, a meal was set out by invisible hands and, as she ate, music played and comforted her soul. In the evening, when she again sat down to eat, she heard roaring as of a wild creature, and she trembled when the beast appeared. But her fear turned to amazement when he asked, very gently, "Dear Beauty, can I stay with you while you eat? I will go away if you prefer, but I would like your company for a while." Beauty was afraid, but nodded her agreement, and the beast remained with her and talked with her as she dined.

The next day was the same as the first, and so time passed, without Beauty being devoured as she had expected. She grew less frightened of the beast, finding him kinder and kinder as the days went by. After a while she was surprised to find that she began to look forward to mealtimes, when the beast would appear and sit with her.

Each evening after their delightful conversation, the beast looked longingly at Beauty and asked her to marry him. "Oh no," she always replied, "though I like you, I could not marry such a beast as you." With that, he always smiled sadly and turned away.

One day, Beauty felt particularly homesick and plucked up courage to ask the beast if it would ever be possible to see her father again, at least to reassure him that she was safe and well cared for.

"Oh Beauty, your request troubles me greatly," the beast replied to her question. "I have grown so fond of having you here and I am afraid that if you leave me, you will forget me. And yet I cannot refuse you your desire. So you may go, only do not forget me, and return after spending a week with your father. So that you do not forget me, take this ring. As soon as you want to come back, put it on your finger and you will be here at once."

Beauty was touched by his response. "Oh thank you, dear, kind beast. Be sure that I will never forget you. I will only be gone for a few days and I promise to return before the week is over."

The merchant was overwhelmed with joy when his daughter suddenly appeared at his fireside. They spent such happy days together that Beauty

completely forgot how long she had been away. She asked her family to remind her when a week had passed, but the sisters plotted to detain her at home, hoping that the monster would devour her if she failed to keep her promise.

However, when she was alone one night, Beauty thought, "How unkind of me to betray the poor beast by staying away so long!" and her sleep was troubled. On the tenth night, she dreamed that she was back in the castle garden and saw the beast lying among the roses, full of grief and calling out to her. Beauty woke grieving and realized how much she missed her beast and how much she wanted to return to him. She remembered the ring he had given her and put it on. Immediately, she found herself back in the dining hall of the castle, where the evening meal was ready for her. "How late he is," she said, as she finished without him. "Perhaps he is angry with me and will never come to me again." She started to hunt for him, but he was nowhere to be found in the castle. Then she remembered her dream. She hurried into the garden and there she saw him, lying forsaken and dying among the roses.

"Dear, dear beast," Beauty cried, throwing herself down beside him and taking his gnarled claws in her hands. "How I have missed you! Please forgive me and smile at me again!"

But the beast lay motionless and pale. She stroked his rough face with her soft hand and he opened his eyes. "Dear Beauty, I thought you had forgotten me and so I am dying, for I can no longer live without you."

"Dear beast! Dear, kind beast! Do not die. Stay with me. I will not leave you again, but live with you here and be your wife." With that, she kissed him tenderly and closed her eyes.

The castle was suddenly filled with lights and music and when Beauty looked again at the beast, he had disappeared. In his place was a young prince, who smiled at her joyfully. "I am the beast whom you feared," he explained. "I was bewitched by an evil fairy and condemned to stay in that monstrous form until a woman could love me. Now I am released from her spell and we can live together in peace."

Beauty's delight was even greater when they entered the castle and found her family there to greet them. The merchant was overcome by his daughter's happiness and embraced both her and her prince with great joy. The envious sisters were turned into stone statues, and so they must remain until they overcome their envy. But Beauty and her prince were married and reigned contentedly in their kingdom for a very long time.

THE GIRL WHO
HELPED THUNDER

MUSKOGEE (NORTH AMERICA)

Long, long ago, there lived a young girl named Brave Heart who had learned to hunt. She used to follow her brothers whenever they went out, despite their attempts to drive her back home. She watched and imitated them and before long became a fine archer, skilled with the bow and arrow.

During the summer months, the people of Brave Heart's tribe lived on fish from the rivers that flowed through their land, and on the corn, beans and squash that grew in the valleys. But when winter came, they depended on meat from the racoons and white-tailed deer for their food. Every year, Brave Heart waited eagerly for the hunting season to start. As the days grew shorter, she spent many hours competing with her brothers at their target-shooting games, often annoying them by winning. More than anything else, she wanted

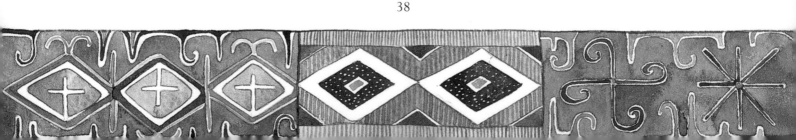

to bring home some meat for her family. She dreamed of being asked by the men of the Muskogee people to go with them on their hunt, but for a long time everyone just laughed at her. Then, one fine autumn day, her dream was fulfilled when her uncles invited her to go with them into the hills.

But you can imagine Brave Heart's disappointment when she realized, as they set up their first camp, that the men expected her to do the cooking while they hunted! She was very upset, but she held back her tears and tackled the job bravely. Before long, the men had all disappeared and she was quite alone. While Brave Heart tended the fire and stirred the meal, she suddenly heard a strange, rumbling thunder. It came not from the sky but from the ground beside and beneath her. She looked around in surprise and then followed the sound to its source, in the stream near the camp. As she approached, she saw a very old man wrestling with a water snake. Thunder roared with each movement as he struggled to free himself. In the midst of the turmoil, she noticed a bright white circle on the snake's neck. As she watched, both man and snake begged her for help.

The old man cried out, "Shoot him! Aim for the white spot on his throat! There is no other way to save me from certain death."

The snake shouted, "Kill the old man before his thunder destroys you. Save me and you will save yourself!"

Brave Heart was very troubled and confused. "Whom should I help?" she wondered. "Oh, what shall I do? If I destroy the thunder, we may lose the rain that he brings with him, and then we will have no corn to eat. I have no choice but to kill the snake." Sadly, she put her arrow on the bowstring and, eyeing the snake's white spot, aimed as carefully as she could. The arrow

flew into the creature's soft flesh; instantly it released the old man from its coils and sank beneath the water.

Old Man Thunder pulled himself out of the stream and came towards Brave Heart smiling. He was shocked to find that she was a young girl. "You are so young and so skillful," he said in amazement, "you will be my friend forever. Your people will soon need help, so listen to me carefully before I leave you."

Brave Heart paid close attention to his words. "Though you are a girl, you must go through the rituals that your brothers practice when they need direction from the spirits. I will teach you a song that will give you great power to help your people, but you must sing it only when necessary."

Shortly afterwards, the men came back to camp and prepared to return to their village, for the hunt had been successful. Brave Heart followed them on the trail and as they walked, she asked her uncles to help her perform the medicine fast, going without food for four days to prepare her spirit for her special task. Her uncles were amused at her urgency. "You are too young! And girls do not need such things anyway."

She persisted in her request, however, and the youngest of her uncles finally said, "I do not understand why you have this thing in your heart, but I will help you, daughter with a brave heart."

In the weeks that followed, he arranged the ceremony, assisting her as an uncle should. All through the difficult nights in the sweat lodge, he stayed beside

her and led her to the place of fasting and prayer. During those four days, she remembered Old Man Thunder's words, "I will teach you a song that will give you great power to help your people," and she felt reassured.

As winter drew nearer and the men were out in the hills hunting for the winter's meat, the Muskogee people learned that Cherokee warriors were pressing towards them. When Brave Heart's uncle heard of this he went to look for his niece. He saw her from a distance, walking towards the east, away from her village. Then she started to move in a large circle around it, and as she walked she sang a strange song. Four times she sang and four times she circled; then she changed her form, evaporating into a beautiful rainbow that formed a huge arc over the village. The uncle watched, full of wonder.

"Look up at the sky!" shouted a Cherokee warrior, as he too saw the mighty rainbow arch above them. Suddenly, from the midst of the rainbow, Brave Heart raised her bow and started to shoot arrows of lightning around the Cherokee warriors as they prepared to attack her village. Her arrows flew and the thunder roared as each one shot through the sky towards the earth. All the Cherokees were easily captured, and they trembled as Brave Heart resumed her girl shape and cried out to them, "Remember what you have seen here today. Now go back to your own villages and tell it to your people and leave us in peace."

All the Cherokee warriors fled at her words and never returned to harm the Muskogee people. Brave Heart had saved her village and her youngest uncle was proud that he had helped her. "We will tell stories about you," he said. "You will be honored for all time as the Girl Who Helped Thunder."

CAP O'RUSHES

ENGLISH

In times gone by, there lived a very rich man who had three beautiful daughters. The eldest was as dark as midnight, the second had eyes as green as a cat's, and the third was as fair as the morning. Their father was devoted to them all, though his youngest daughter was his favorite.

One day, he returned from the city with three marvelous gowns as gifts for his daughters. The first was covered with rubies, the second with emeralds, and the third with smooth, white pearls. "Try on your new dresses," he urged them, "and let me see how beautiful you look."

The sisters ran off excitedly to dress themselves and returned in splendor to their father. They curtsied before him and he was most pleased with them. "Do you really like your gifts?" he kept asking, and they thanked him again and again. "Thank you, dearest father," they said, "we are always grateful for your

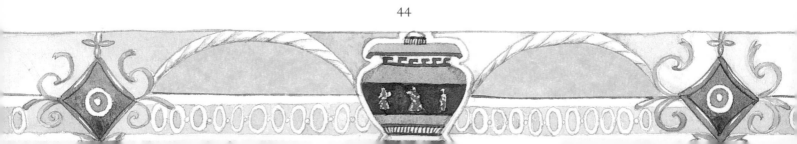

generous presents." They kissed him repeatedly as the evening sky darkened over the hills outside.

"Am I a kind father to you, my dears?" he asked, to which they always replied with laughter. Then he spoke more urgently. "My lovely daughters, do you really think that I am a good father to you?"

"Most certainly, father! The kindest father in the whole world," answered the dark sister.

"Dearest father," replied the green-eyed sister, "you are all that a daughter could hope for."

But the youngest sister remained silent, deeply contented with her gift.

Their father was still unsatisfied, and persisted with his questions. "But how much do you love me? Can you tell me that?"

The dark sister caught sight of herself in her rich gown in a mirror, and responded, "Dear father, I love you as much as life itself." Her father beamed and turned to his green-eyed daughter as she gazed into the emeralds on her gown.

"Dearest father, I love you more than the whole world holds." He heard her with pleasure and then drew the fairest of his daughters to him and repeated his question.

"Truly, my father," she replied, "I love you as much as fresh meat loves salt."

Her father was disappointed and angry at such an answer and begged her to say more, but she stood silently before him. He grew angrier and raged, "So, you do not really love me and do not value my gifts. Then be off with you! Go out into the world and see what you can find without me." With that he opened the door and she went out into the night without a word.

A serving maid came after her to give her an old cloak for cover and a lantern to find her way. With these she set off into the night and walked till morning, when she found herself at the gates of a palace, much grander than her father's house. The tired girl found a stream nearby and pulled up rushes and grasses to make herself a rough garment. She took off her gown and wrapped it in the ragged cloak and went to the kitchen door to ask for work. The housekeeper pitied her and took her in, instructing her to scrub the floor straightaway. The other servants were amused by the new servant girl's appearance and called her Cap O'Rushes. And so the poor girl began her lowly life.

Some weeks later, it was announced that the king was to hold a ball, to which all eligible young women were to be invited so that the prince might choose a bride. The servants worked all day to prepare a fine feast, and they were told that they might wash and dress up and watch the dancing from the gallery. Cap O'Rushes pretended to be tired and went straight to bed while all the other servants ran off to watch the ball. But as soon as she was alone, she took out her satin gown sewn with pearls and gold thread, put it on and went to the ball. All who saw her were amazed at her beauty.

"Will you please dance with me?" the prince asked, time after time throughout the evening. At the end of the ball, he was distressed to find that she had vanished the moment he had turned his back.

"How splendid the ball was," the servants reported next morning. "You should have been there, Cap O'Rushes, to see the most beautiful princess, dressed in a beautiful gown of satin and pearls. The prince would dance with no one else."

Determined to meet the princess again, the prince requested that another ball be given the next night. Again Cap O'Rushes feigned tiredness and went to the ball secretly, while the servants watched from the gallery. The mysterious princess came and danced all evening, and this time the prince put on her finger an old, golden ring set with pearls, as a token of his love. Next morning, the servants again reported the events of the night before, excitedly telling of the beautiful princess in the gown bejeweled with pearls.

"She is a foreign princess," they said, "and no one knows who she is. But the prince would dance only with her. Again she disappeared as suddenly as she came, and no one knows where to find her."

The prince was so distressed at losing his princess a second time that he held yet another ball. Everyone longed to see the foreign princess in her marvelous gown dancing all evening with the prince. Once more she appeared. Once more she danced, then disappeared as mysteriously as she came, returning to her attic and hiding her dress as on the other nights. The servants reported that the princess had again eluded the prince, who was desperate with sadness.

In his yearning for his lost princess, the prince became pale. Day after day, he searched the countryside, enquiring of rich and poor whether anyone knew where he could find his dancing partner in the gown of pearls. But she was nowhere to be found and the prince became sicker and sicker with longing for the princess.

"The prince will die soon if the princess is not found," the servants confided to Cap O'Rushes. "He will eat nothing and gets weaker and weaker, wishing only that he might die, for he says he cannot live without her."

Cap O'Rushes went to the housekeeper and said, "I know a very special gruel that will strengthen the prince. Let me make some for him."

The housekeeper agreed, and the young girl made her gruel and dropped the ring of pearls into it. The housekeeper took the bowl to the prince's chamber and he ate it hungrily. At the bottom of the dish he found the ring. His heart pounded as he asked the housekeeper who had made his gruel.

"A young girl who is working in the kitchen," the housekeeper replied.

"I must see her at once!" the prince cried. "Send her to me now."

Cap O'Rushes quickly put on her gown beneath her cloak and entered the prince's chamber. He took her hand and placed the ring on her finger, and it fit perfectly. Cap O'Rushes threw off the old cloak and stood before him in all

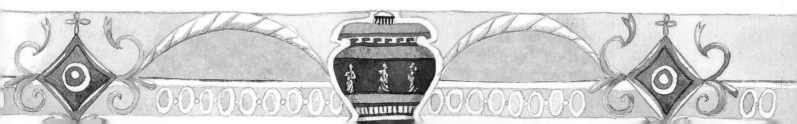

her splendor. They embraced and vowed never to be parted again. Their marriage was announced immediately and preparations for the feast began.

The young bride asked her prince, "Please invite my father to the wedding, but do not tell him who is to be your bride."

The prince did as she asked, and the old man made his way to the palace. He had long repented his angry and cruel treatment of his daughter and had wandered alone throughout the country trying to find her. His other daughters had taken their fortune and abandoned him while he was off searching for his wronged child. Wearily he came to the wedding feast and sat at the lowest table of all.

The bride had instructed the cook to prepare two separate meals. The first was to be cooked without any salt and the other was to be prepared with salt as usual. So the feast began and the saltless meal was served. It looked magnificent, but when all the guests tasted it, they grimaced and refused to eat more than one mouthful, for the food lacked flavor.

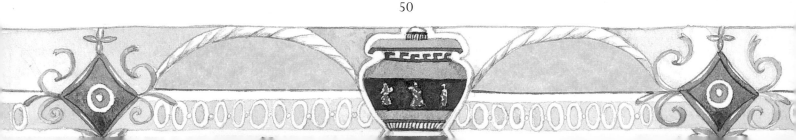

The old man sat silent, full of grief for his lost daughter. He looked at the radiant bride and cried out in amazement as he realized he was looking at his long-lost daughter. He quickly rose from his place and approached her. He kissed her gently and turned to speak to the guests.

"Dear friends," he began, "I have been a very foolish father." Then he told everyone how he had demanded to know how much his daughters loved him, and what his youngest daughter's response had been. "'I love you as much as fresh meat loves salt,' she told me, and I did not understand. But now I know what she meant, and I realize that she loves me dearly." He turned to his daughter and begged her forgiveness.

"Dearest father," she responded, "of course I forgive you. I only ask you to rejoice with me in my happiness and celebrate with us at our wedding feast."

"Gladly will I rejoice with you both," her father replied. And as he sat down with them the second meal was brought in. This food was more delicious than you can imagine and everyone feasted on it with joy.

SAVITRI AND SATYAVAN

INDIAN

Long ago, there lived in India a king and queen who yearned for a child. Finally, after many barren years, a daughter was born, bringing them much joy. They gave her the name Savitri. They watched her grow up with delight, and almost before they realized it, she became a lovely young woman.

Not only was Savitri beautiful to look at; she was also quick and clever, with a great talent for solving riddles and puzzles.

One day, her father said to her, "Savitri, it is time for you to find a partner, for you must leave us and start a family of your own. Tell me which young man you desire for a husband."

Savitri had known that this day must come and she had often thought about it. So she said to her father, "I have looked around me and so far I have not yet seen any man who attracts me, who makes me want to share my life with him."

The king was disappointed at these words and wondered whether her life had been too sheltered, living so happily with her parents in their court. So he responded, "I shall send throughout the country for pictures of every young man who might make a suitable husband for you. In this way, your eye may find him, for the heart speaks through the face." So he sent his court painters throughout the kingdom to make likenesses of all of the noble men they could find. When this was done, Savitri carefully studied the pictures, but none of the faces attracted her.

The king was dismayed, but he did not give up, saying, "Perhaps you need to go out into the world and see it for yourself. Then you will meet someone who touches your heart."

Savitri was pleased with this suggestion and her excitement mounted as she watched her father assemble camels, elephants and horses to transport and accompany her on her search. For many months she traveled, searching through all the cities in the world, facing all the dangers and enjoying all the pleasures of her journey. But nowhere could she find a man to love.

She returned to her father's kingdom discouraged, but the king would not admit defeat. "You have sought your lover in the cities of men with no success. But the world contains more than great cities, so you must prepare yourself to set out once more. This time, you must enter the dark forests and search there for a man you can love."

Again the king gathered together camels and elephants and horses to carry the princess and her companions on their journey and he encouraged his daughter, as she set off, with warm words, "Be courageous and open your heart to love in the deep forests of the world."

For many months, Savitri journeyed from forest to forest, never finding the one who could touch her heart. She was ready to return home as she entered the last, unknown forest. But there in the midst of the trees she came across a young woodcutter swinging his axe. She greeted him kindly.

"My name is Princess Savitri," she said. "Who are you?"

"I am Satyavan, your Royal Highness," he answered.

They began to talk, and he answered all her questions, explaining that his parents were old and blind. "Each day I chop wood for their fire, then I collect and cook their food," he said. "That is how I spend my life."

The princess was touched by his story and for the first time she felt love in her heart. She returned to her father, joyfully telling him of her discovery.

54

After he had heard her story, the king said, "But the man is very poor, living in a simple cottage at the edge of the forest. Do you think you could share such a life with him and be happy?"

"I do not care for wealth, for rich foods, clothes or jewels," Savitri replied. "I want to spend my life with Satyavan, however poor he may be."

The king was pleased his daughter had found someone to love, and sent his messengers to the blind, old couple to inform them that the princess would marry their son. When Satyavan came home from working in the forest all day, they told him the news. At first he was sad. "I have nothing to offer this princess," he exclaimed. "She is wealthy, I am poor. I love her, but she cannot possibly live in this poor cottage with me."

His parents comforted him by telling him their story, kept secret until now. "Dear son," his mother said, "you are also a prince. You are worthy of the beautiful Savitri."

"My brother plotted against me and took my kingdom from me by deceit," his father continued. "Then, having robbed me of my birthright, he blinded us both and left us to survive as best we could in the forest."

Satyavan was amazed and he rejoiced that he could marry a king's daughter. So the wedding was arranged. The king was so delighted that his daughter had found her bridegroom, that he prepared a magnificent celebration.

It happened that a very old sage attended the wedding. He came to the king and warned him against the marriage. "It would be a terrible mistake," he said, "for although Satyavan is a most brave and kind young man, his destiny is to die very soon. He cannot escape his destiny."

The king despaired when he heard this. He called Savitri to him and told her of the sage's tragic prophecy.

"I fear nothing and I wish to marry Satyavan," she insisted. "Together we shall face whatever life brings." However, she was a wise young woman and she asked the sage whether there might be some remedy for Satyavan's fate. The sage thought long and hard and then said, "You can spare his life for just twelve months, if you eat only fruits and berries of the forest. But then he will die. That is the only hope I can offer you."

The marriage was celebrated and Savitri began her simple life in the forest with Satyavan and his parents. Day after day, she fasted, which gave some concern to her new family. But she always laughed and said, "Do not worry about me. I am very well and I eat those things I enjoy most."

So her fast continued, and on the very last day of the year, she got up in the morning and said, "Today I will come with you into the forest." Satyavan and his parents tried to dissuade her, but she insisted. "I am not afraid of the wild animals or the discomforts of the woods," she said. "Remember that I traveled through all the forests in the world in search of you!"

They set off together and soon they came to the very heart of the forest. Savitri's heart was beating and she was afraid, for she knew it was the year's end. Satyavan climbed a large tree and was sawing its branches when, suddenly, he lost his balance and fell. Pale with shock, Savitri helped him to the shade of an old banyan tree. There Satyavan lay, with his head in his wife's lap. And there he died.

Savitri sat in silent grief, till she heard someone approaching. She looked up and saw Yamraj, the King of the Underworld, riding towards her on a water buffalo. He had come to take Satyavan's soul. As he drew near, Savitri gazed up into the banyan tree and cried out, "Dearest banyan tree, I leave my husband's body in your shade. Protect him for me. One day I will return to bring him home."

Savitri then left the cool shade and began to follow Yamraj on foot. For hours and days she walked behind him, until eventually he turned round to face her, saying, "Woman, why do you follow me? Go home."

Savitri replied, "You are taking away the soul of my beloved. Since I cannot live without him, take me with you. Otherwise, I will continue to pursue you."

Yamraj was annoyed and repeated, "Go home, woman. Go home."

Savitri ignored his words and trailed after him until he turned to her and said, "I will grant you one wish to be rid of you. But you must not ask for your husband's soul."

Calmly, Savitri replied, "Please restore the sight of my husband's parents."

Yamraj agreed to give back the old people's sight, urging Savitri to leave him alone. Still she did not go home, but walked after him for many more miles. Yamraj cried out angrily, "I will not be followed! I will grant you another wish, then you must go away. But you cannot ask for Satyavan's soul."

"Please restore the kingdom to my husband's father, that is my wish."

"Very well," Yamraj said, "I will do that. But now you must go home."

So the kingdom was restored to Satyavan's parents, but still Savitri did not turn back. After many more miles Yamraj shouted in exasperation, "I will endure this no longer. I have given you two wishes and still you pursue me. Now I will offer you a third and last wish. Remember, you must not ask for your husband's soul."

With a pounding heart Savitri asked, "Please let me be the mother of many children."

Yamraj replied quickly, desperate to be rid of her, "Yes, yes. You will be the mother of many children. Now stop following me!"

Even then Savitri did not go home. Yamraj could still hear her footsteps behind him. In a fury he shouted at her, "I have granted you all of your wishes, but you still continue to pester me. You have the promise of many children. Why do you follow me still?"

"But how can I have children?" Savitri demanded. "For you are carrying off my dead husband's soul. How then can that wish be fulfilled? You have played false with me."

Yamraj was by now exhausted. "All right!" he exclaimed. "You can have your husband's soul back. Now leave me alone."

Savitri immediately left him and raced back to the banyan tree where Satyavan's body lay in the cool shade. There his soul was restored. Then Savitri and Satyavan embraced. They walked back home joyfully, only Savitri knowing that a surprise awaited them there.

59

THE BEAR IN
THE FOREST HUT

POLISH

There was once an old woodcutter who married a widow. Each of them had a daughter who resembled her parent. The old man's daughter was hardworking and kind, but the widow's child was mean and lazy. The woodcutter loved his daughter dearly, but he was afraid of his new wife and never stood up to her.

The old woman treated her stepdaughter very cruelly and wanted to be rid of her. As winter came and the food supply dwindled, she told her husband that he must take his daughter out into the forest and leave her to fend for herself. So, with his heart full of sorrow, he rode with his daughter into the depths of the forest and abandoned her.

60

For a time, the girl fed on wild strawberries and a piece of dry bread that her father had given her, but she soon became tired and cold. As she wandered deeper into the forest she came across a small hut. She knocked on the door to ask the owner for shelter, but there was no reply. In desperation she tried the doorknob and to her joy the door opened with ease. She went inside and saw that there was a spinning wheel and a pile of flax set out by the window. Grateful at finding a warm refuge, she immediately sat down and began to spin. As she worked she heard a voice singing softly:

Wanderer, wanderer all forlorn, lost in darkness 'til the morn,

If your heart is full of light, rest here safely through the night.

Outside she heard the wind blow through the trees. Suddenly a bear entered the hut and greeted her kindly. "Good evening to you too," she replied nervously.

"Why are you here?" the bear asked. "Have you been brought by force or have you come freely?"

The girl began to cry and as she told her story, the bear stroked her face with his paw. When she had finished he said, "Cry no more. You will be happy again, but you must do as I say and ask no questions. First, you must spin the flax into thread, then you must weave the thread into cloth, then you must make the cloth into a shirt. It must be ready tomorrow night. If it is complete, all will be well." With that he departed, leaving the girl alone in the hut in the dark forest.

By the light of the moon, she finished the spinning, and then she slept for a time. As soon as the sun rose, she went to the stream to wash her face.

When she returned to the hut, she found breakfast set out for her. Once

she had satisfied her hunger, she sat at the loom and weaved till noon. Then she sprinkled the cloth with water from the stream and bleached it in the sun. Finally, she sewed the lovely cloth that she had made into a fine shirt. By evening, the shirt was ready.

When the bear came he was delighted with the shirt, and when he had thanked her he asked for some porridge. While the girl prepared it, he went to fetch his bedding. In the kitchen, a hungry little mouse appeared, begging for some food. The girl gave it some porridge and it scurried off.

The bear came back with his bedding and a pile of stones. After eating his porridge, he said, "Take this bunch of keys and keep jingling them all night." Immediately he fell asleep and the poor girl started to walk around jingling the keys, getting more and more tired. Suddenly the mouse appeared and said, "Give me the keys and I will jingle them for you, for you need to rest. Lie behind the stove where you will be safe."

Gratefully the girl lay down to rest, but she was soon woken by the bear who called out, "Are you alive?"

As she replied, "Yes, I am alive," he started to hurl the rocks around the room. But still the little mouse went on jingling the keys. And so they spent the night.

As soon as the cock crowed, the mouse gave the keys back to the girl and she jingled them till the bear woke. Seeing the girl, he exclaimed, "Dear daughter of the old woodcutter, I bless you! Because of you, I will soon become a man again. I was once a rich king, but I was changed into a bear by a spell that could only be broken if some loving soul would spend two nights in this hut. Now it is nearly over, and I ask you to be my bride and will take you with me to my kingdom. But first, please look into my right ear."

The happy girl peered into the bear's ear and saw a beautiful country, full of mountains and green valleys. She saw flocks of sheep and thriving towns and villages. "That is my kingdom," the bear said, "and you will be its queen. Now look into my left ear."

Then she looked into his left ear and saw a splendid castle, horses and carriages, rich clothes and jewels. "Which of the carriages do you like best?" the bear asked.

The girl replied, "The silver coach with the four white horses."

The bear assured her, "That will be yours. And now you must wait, for your father will come to find you. You must go home with him in your carriage." At these words, she found herself richly clothed and heard the sound of a coach arriving outside the hut. The bear disappeared, and the girl saw her father outside the hut, for he had come searching for her. As they drove up to their poor cottage in the silver coach, the dog began to bark:

Bow! Wow! Wow! The rich girl's here, guarded by her father dear.

She glows with gold and gowns of silk, in a coach with horses white as milk.

The old wife was amazed when she saw her stepdaughter so richly dressed and pretended to be kind to her, asking how she had found such treasure. Of course, she was plotting the same fate for her own daughter. The next morning, the old woman sent her husband off with her own daughter, who was left in the same place and found the same hut. While she waited for the bear she, too, heard the words:

Wanderer, wanderer all forlorn, lost in darkness till the morn,

If your heart is full of light, rest here safely through the night.

The greedy girl grinned at the bear who came into the hut, for she had no fear of him now that she knew what had happened to her stepsister, and hardly

listened as he told her that he needed a shirt by the next evening. The next day
she did no work at all and did not even reply to his inquiries about the shirt.
When he asked her to make porridge, the same hungry mouse appeared, but she
threw the spoon at it. The bear came back, ate the porridge and settled down to
sleep, instructing her that she must jingle the keys all night. Soon he was
snoring. The girl lay down nearby to rest. When the bear called out, "Are you
alive?" she woke abruptly and reached for the keys. But as she did so a huge stone
hit her and killed her in one blow.

At sunrise, the bear woke up and stood on the threshold, stamping his feet 'til
the hut trembled. As he stamped, he was transformed into a king, with a golden
crown on his head. A golden carriage drew up outside, pulled by six
sun-colored horses, and the king stepped inside.

The king ordered his coachman to drive straight to the woodcutter's cottage.
There he embraced his bride. As they left the woodcutter's home, the coachman
cracked his whip. At this, the old house fell apart and only a ruin remained. The
king carried his queen back to his castle where they lived happily for many years.
The woodcutter went with them, and in his old age, he became wiser in his
daughter's kingdom.

THE INVISIBLE GRANDFATHER

ITALIAN

There was once a poor, fatherless girl who lived in poverty with her mother and two sisters. One day she said to her family, "I can't stay here any longer in this hut with nothing to eat. I am going to set out to make a place for myself in the world." And so she left, with nothing but the rags on her back.

After walking for many miles, just when she felt she could walk no further, she came to a palace. To her surprise, the door was wide open. "I will go straight in," she thought, "for they might need a servant." She went in and since no one came to receive her, she called out, "Is there anyone at home to give work to a poor girl?" Her call echoed through the great halls and no one replied. She

66

discovered the kitchens and there in the cupboards she found some bread and rice and a little wine. "This is enough for a feast," she said.

As soon as she spoke, two hands appeared to lay the table. Then they prepared a delicious meal for her. "How lucky I am," the girl thought, as she sat down to eat. When she had finished, she said to herself, "How satisfied I feel now. But I am so tired after my journey. I would like to sleep."

She wandered through the palace looking for a place to rest. She found a room with a beautiful canopied bed, such as she had never seen before. "How good it would be to sleep in that!" she exclaimed, "beneath such soft sheets." She lay down and the next thing she knew, it was already morning.

As soon as she awoke, the same two hands that had prepared her evening meal brought her breakfast, and after she had satisfied her morning hunger, she started to explore the lonely palace again. Finding wardrobes full of beautiful gowns, she threw her rags aside and put on a jeweled dress. Then she caught sight of herself in a mirror. "How beautiful I look!" she exclaimed. And indeed, she did look far more lovely than in her rags.

Wearing her fine clothes, she walked out into the garden just as a king drove by in his carriage. When he saw this lovely young woman, his heart was touched and he longed to talk with her. He stopped his carriage and approached her, plying her with many questions. "Good morning, sweet lady. Please tell me your name? Whose palace is this? Whose daughter are you?" And he asked permission to visit her again.

The girl was impressed by his courtesy and replied, "I have no parents but if you will return here another day, I will have answers to your questions." The king bowed low and left in his carriage.

The girl returned indoors and went straight to the huge fireplace in the center of the great hall. Curious to find out about the lonely palace, she began to talk to the fireplace. "Kind sir," she pleaded, "I don't know where I am or how I found this place. Though I can see no one, I have been well provided for and I am deeply grateful. But please tell me what I must do, for a king wishes to court me."

To her surprise, a deep voice spoke from the chimney. "Beautiful you are and even more beautiful you will become. Receive my blessing and do as I say. Tell the king that your grandfather who is sick and lonely is happy for you to marry, only you must not delay. Go to him with this message, most lovely girl whose loveliness will increase."

The next day when the king called for his reply, he found that the girl had grown more lovely than he remembered. She called to him from her balcony, "My grandfather is willing for you to court me, as long as the marriage is not delayed." The king was delighted and they spent many hours talking together.

The next week passed, and then the girl went to the chimney again and asked, "Dear Grandfather, do you think that we have courted long enough, and that we may now marry?"

The grandfather replied, "Beautiful you are and even more beautiful you will become! Yes, it is time to marry. But when you leave, you must be absolutely sure to take with you every single item that is in the palace. Leave nothing behind, most lovely girl whose loveliness will increase."

The girl swept out the palace and removed everything. But she forgot to take the necklace that she planned to wear. When the carriage arrived to bear her away, she went to the fireplace and said, "Dearest Grandfather, now I will leave

you, for my bridegroom has come for me. I have done all you asked me to do. The palace is empty and I will depart."

"Thank you," the deep voice replied. "Now leave me alone."

So the girl left with her bridegroom, who was again amazed that her beauty was greater than ever. But as they drove away, the girl suddenly remembered the necklace that she had planned to wear and she insisted that they go back to retrieve it. She rushed back into the palace and called out to the fireplace, "Dear Grandfather, I am so sorry but I forgot one thing: the necklace that I intended to wear. I have come back for it."

An angry voice cried out to her as she put the gold chain around her neck, "Be off with you, you ugly, bearded woman!" As soon as the words were spoken, she felt her face become hairy and found she had grown a beard that reached down to her waist. In terror she ran out to her bridegroom who was also horrified by what he saw. "I can't take you back to my castle like this!" he said. "We must go to my house in the forest and decide what to do."

Each day the king came to the forest to visit his betrothed, to bring her food and drink and speak with her. Rumors soon spread that he was courting an ugly, bearded woman. But the king still loved her.

One day the girl said to the king, "Please bring me a black velvet dress and a black veil to cover my face, for I must go to speak with my grandfather again." The clothes were brought to her, and the girl drove back to the palace. She approached the fireplace cautiously. "Grandfather," she whispered, "it's me."

"You hideous thing! What do you want from me?" he replied gruffly.

"Dear Grandfather, hear me," she begged. "Because I am bearded, my life is at stake. You are responsible for my grief."

"Me, responsible?" he repeated. "You were the one to leave something behind when I told you that everything must be taken away from the palace."

But the girl persisted, "O Grandfather, be merciful! I do not ask for the beauty you gave me, the beauty that increased each day as I lived in your palace. All I ask is that I become the girl I was when I first came here. Grandfather, please help me and make me the way I used to be."

The grandfather heard her pleas and relented. "Very well, so it will be. But you are certain that you have not left anything behind this time?"

"Oh no," she cried, "I have the necklace in my hand and the palace is quite, quite empty."

Now a gentle, deep voice echoed from the chimney, "Beautiful you are and even more beautiful you will become. Go and marry your king, most lovely girl whose loveliness will increase."

She ran back to her beloved with her beauty renewed. The king was overjoyed and he took her back to his castle, where the whole kingdom rejoiced at his good fortune. The two were married and then they appeared before their people who shouted, "Long live our new king and queen."

SHEHERAZADE

ARABIAN

It is recorded in the chronicles of times long past, that there reigned in Arabia a king called Shah Shehriyar. For some years, the Shah and his wife lived happily. Then his wife betrayed him. Full of bitterness and anger, Shah Shehriyar swore that he would never remarry, but to ensure that he was not deceived again he demanded that a young woman visit him each night, and be slain the next morning. He instructed his vizier to find these women for him, and threatened him with his life if he failed to obey.

This dreadful deed was performed day after day and the citizens grew to fear their Shah. Fathers and mothers cried out against his fury. But nothing could assuage his fierce anger. Soon there were only two maidens left in the city. And these were the daughters of the vizier himself.

When the vizier had searched in vain for one last maiden, he feared his audience with Shah Shehriyar, for if the Shah's rage was not satisfied, he knew he would lose his head. In his anxiety, he confided in his daughters, Sheherazade and Dunyazade. They were very alarmed to hear his news and feared for their lives. Sheherazade was silent for a while. She was a brave and clever young woman who had read all the stories of her people and had become extremely knowledgeable and wise.

"Father, I am most distressed about what has happened to the innocent young women in this kingdom," she said. "There must be a way to end this cruel tyranny." After some thought, she continued, "I myself will go to our Shah! Take me to him, and I will deliver us all from his vengeance."

"In the name of Allah," cried out her father, "do not speak so foolishly. You would perish as all the others have perished."

But all she would say was, "It must be so. It will be so."

The vizier used every argument he could think of to make her put this notion out of her head, but her heart was set on the enterprise and all she would say was, "It must be so. It will be so."

Then she added, "If you do not take me to the Shah, I will go alone and tell him that you refuse to bring me to fulfill his demands," and the vizier no longer dared deny her request.

Before she went to the Shah, Sheherazade told her sister Dunyazade, "Be sure to be alert tonight. When the Shah sends for you, come quickly. When I greet you, ask me to tell you a story to pass away the night before I must lose my head."

With that she gave herself to the Shah, who was delighted by her beauty and wit. But after he had lain with her, she began to weep, and when he asked what

troubled her, she said, "Since I must die tomorrow, I would like to see my sister Dunyazade for the last time."

The Shah sent for Dunyazade at once and she came as planned, greeting her sister with affectionate tears and saying, "Dear Sister, let us spend this sad night together in the telling of stories. It will help pass the time till dawn."

With the Shah's permission, Sheherazade began her tale:

"In times past, there was a merchant who was rich beyond compare. As he traveled through a hot country, he came upon a most beautiful garden and he sat beneath a walnut tree to enjoy its shade. Suddenly..."

And so the story began, and the Shah listened eagerly as Sheherazade's beautiful voice rose and fell, now with sorrow and now with excitement. She went on spinning her tale until she saw the light begin to glow through the window. When she stopped, the Shah was most disappointed.

"What a marvelous tale!" he exclaimed. "Never have I heard the like."

"By Allah," Sheherazade replied, "this tale is nothing compared to the one I would relate tomorrow night. Only, since I must die with the morning light, that cannot be."

"We must hear another tale this coming night," the Shah decided, and he called in his vizier. "Be sure to let Sheherazade rest this day, for I will hear another story tonight."

The vizier and his daughters rejoiced at the reprieve, which was only one of many, for so began the first of a thousand and one tales told by Sheherazade to entertain the Shah.

Night after night the Shah was moved by Sheherazade's stories and he could

never bear to let her go. During those thousand and one nights, she bore him three children. Then at first light one morning, she said to the Shah, "O Shah, for these many nights I have entertained you with tales of magic and love. I have recounted histories and stories of war and wisdom, and now I have a request. May I ask just one favor?"

"Most surely, fair Sheherazade, ask me what you will and by Allah I will grant your request."

"Please bring my children to me," she said. When the nurses brought the children to the Shah's apartments, Sheherazade said boldly, "O Shah, these are your children. I beg that you will spare me so that I can take care of them and give them the love of a mother and raise strong sons and daughters."

Then Shah Shehriyar spoke solemnly to her. "Most precious and clever Sheherazade, I pardoned you even before these children were born, for you are generous and fair and deserve to live long. You have wooed me with wit and wisdom and with the magic of your stories, and I beg you to marry me with feasting and rejoicing, that all may honor you."

And so it was announced and the kingdom was filled with the music and laughter of the wedding feast. The vizier was overjoyed that his daughter was spared, and even more that her wisdom had saved the innocent and won the heart and mind of Shah Shehriyar.

So praise be to Allah who is not wasted by time; who will give peace and grant us, and all stories, a good end.

NOTES

THE KING'S DAUGHTER

 The personal and social state of the father marks his daughter, who goes out into the world under his banner. Though this may be restrictive, it gives her an initial identity and place in life. If we read the tales symbolically and not as sociological documents, we can experience how it feels to be a king's daughter, like Savitri, who feels her royal value even in a poor woodcutter's cottage, or a poor farmer's daughter, or even an orphan. The tales offer us vivid possibilities that accord with our shifting sense of self, our moods and different phases of our development. To be impoverished, or to feel imprisoned in a cow barn like Aluel, is disabling and creates obstacles that must be overcome before we can go forward and forge our own identity.

The identity and role of the father was once much more clearly defined and less complicated than it is today, and perhaps less rich in possibilities. The changing expectations of fatherhood in the modern world creates much insecurity. Perhaps folktales can help us to clarify what is essential and what is negotiable in the father-daughter relationship.

FATHER AS PROTECTOR AND PROVIDER

 These stories often disturb the simple trust on the part of the daughter and father that she can be sheltered from the dangers of life. The daughter's belief that her father will protect her, even from her own fear, is shattered in *The Frog Prince*.

Overprotective fathers damage their daughters' potential just as decisively as fathers who actively hinder and destroy the daughter's own capacity to act. The father's task is to encourage the girl's sense of purpose and power, her goals, ambitions and desires, and her right to pursue them. Fathers traditionally provide "daily bread" and when all is well, this can be taken for granted emotionally as well as literally. Often fathers also assert their largesse with special presents, and daughters such as Cap O'Rushes need to discriminate between what is a genuine gift and what is manipulation.

The worst crisis for the daughter is to be thrown from her father's care; but once expelled, Cap O'Rushes survives on her wits and discovers a life far richer than a father could provide. Similarly, the woodcutter in *The Bear in the Forest* abandons his child in the forest, where she works effectively at her destiny in the depths of her own inner world (perhaps the meaning or one of the implications of "the great forest").

FATHER AND MARRIAGE

 The daughter is fruit of the father's romance with the mother, and for him the daughter inevitably carries fond memories of his wife. This is explicit in *Aluel and her Loving Father* and in *The Green Knight*, when the mother dies and the child fills the emotional void. Since mothers often used to die in childbirth, they frequently expressed fear for their children at the hands of the husband's new wife and these tales enact that anxiety. But remarriage is a risk that must be taken, for the daughter cannot offer the same love for a father as a wife can.

While incestuous longings hover round some of these tales, marriage outside the family is strictly enforced and the good father ensures that his daughter leaves him to unite with a man other than himself. In the Italian tale, the invisible grandfather promotes the girl's marriage, and he insists that he be left alone when she becomes queen of her new kingdom. Savitri's father also knows that a partner exists for his daughter and enables her to find him.

The daughter's preoccupation with the father is often indicated by her own reluctance to marry; Beauty says explicitly that she is not ready to leave her father. Since marriage in fairy tales may symbolize letting go of the father, the refusal to marry must be overcome. However, this does not imply that the daughter ceases to develop as a woman on her own terms.

THE BEWITCHED PRINCE

The prince is usually the carrier of renewed masculine energy, rich and potent as is expected of the next ruler of the kingdom. Often, because of the weakness in his father and/or possessiveness on the part of his mother, the prince has been in some way bewitched and has to be rescued from such imprisonment. Since it is easy for the daughter to be seduced back into the realm of nature and to refuse creative tasks beyond the biological, it is vital that her "prince" — as part of her own inner reality — should recover his human qualities and be strong in order to balance the powerful world of the mother.

FEELING AND TRANSFORMATION

In *Beauty and the Beast*, the red rose Beauty requests from her father and his desire to find one for her establish a potentially erotic collusion, since the red rose is the flower of love. The rose grows in the beast's garden and is rightly *his* gift to Beauty. There is dangerous energy constellated in this tale and Beauty eventually has to choose between father and lover. The beast is transformed only when Beauty can embrace the male animal. Beauty's beast is both a beastly and a spiritual creature; these aspects must unite in one being and not be split into two separate relationships.

In *The Frog Prince*, transformation is also brought about by an explosion of feeling; not the tenderness that overwhelms Beauty, but sheer rage and horror. Emotion, like fire, is the energy behind transformations in fairy tales. The Polish woodcutter's daughter encounters an intimidating, rock-hurling bear, who compensates for an ineffectual, hen-pecked father. The positive aggressive energy of the bear, that would enable a weak man to stand up to a dominating wife, is integrated by the bear-prince and then humanized as a prince, whose strength can be put at the service of his wife and kingdom.

AUTHORITY AND TRADITION

Fairy tales frequently illustrate the folly of fathers and the wisdom of daughters. Fathers often have to be taught and even redeemed by their daughters. Here, the tales are most subversive, particularly those deriving from strict patriarchal societies. Authority is shown to be flawed and defied with good cause. The foolish father in *Cap O'Rushes* has to be taught what love is and what boundaries father-daughter love requires. This lesson is taught by means of a mundane reality — the salting of meat.

FATHER AND CULTURE

In fairy tales, fathers often embody the authority and wisdom of culture, and traditional and moral values. Fathers are expected to introduce a moral code into their daughters' lives, thus creating a sense of security. The tales both enforce and sabotage this security. Sheherazade shares her father's values; he has encouraged her wit and her familiarity with poetry and history. Sheherazade's quickness of mind and spirit, like Savitri's, seems to have been nourished by her relationship with her father.

The world of the father is a world of thought, of principle, of honor, action and political necessity. In this world, the power of the word is tremendous and in the oral tradition the spoken word is as potent as the written. This is the territory of the contract, the prohibition, and its laws are absolute — even promises to frogs must be honored.

SURROGATE FATHERS

Kings and Shahs are fathers to their kingdoms and this bond has some of the complexity of individual father-daughter dynamics, especially in the use and abuse of power. Sheherazade transforms the Shah by her wit and tenderness.

In some cultures, uncles play a vital role. The uncle as facilitator is vividly illustrated in *The Girl Who Helped Thunder*. Brave Heart's uncle helps her fulfill her mission, crossing gender boundaries and adopting traditionally male roles.

In the absence of a father, the daughter typically creates a grandiose father-figure. Such is the invisible grandfather of the Italian story. He not only provides materially, more importantly he affirms psychologically. An inflated sense of beauty has to be moderated however, and the poor girl has to be willing to embrace her ordinary reality. Then the fatherless daughter becomes the king's bride.

Yamaraj, King of the Underworld, carries destructive energy. His power is challenged by the confident "king's daughter," who is able to trick him and claim life.

FURTHER READING

Folk and fairy tales were not written down or regarded as literature until the late 17th century. They were seen as part of a popular oral tradition, peasant tales for hearth or spinning room. When tales such as *Beauty and the Beast* came to prominence among aristocratic women in Paris, the stories became socially acceptable. The recorded tales, like those gathered and embellished by Charles Perrault, were far more sophisticated than the rawer peasant tales that were later taken from the lips of people all over the world.

There are numerous 19th century collections of fairy tales from around the world. See especially the work of Joseph Jacobs, such as his *Celtic Fairy Tales*. The collections by the Grimm brothers purported to be taken verbatim from rural tellers, but we know now that they did a lot of editing. A good translation of the Grimm tales is by Padraic Colum. The Folklore Library (University College London and Warburg) is the most abundant and international collection of folk literature, where most of these tales were found. Some of them are still in print in collections made by Andrew Lang. There are now many North American native peoples' collections. Many were originally collected by missionaries, with their inevitable biases. But later they were collected and transcribed by cultural anthropologists and literary collectors. That is also true of Asian Indian stories and myths.

Most 19th century interest was from philologists, cultural anthropologists and folklorists. In the 20th century, psychologists recognized the relevance of these tales to universal human psychology, including Jung, Freud, Bettelheim and Marie Louise von Franz. They are now even used by medical psychiatrists.

Literary scholars have studied fairy tales, including Max Luthi in Zurich, Vladimir Propp in Russia and many subsequent commentators. Stith Thompson famously cataloged universal motifs found in fairy tales.

Barefoot Books

step inside a story

At Barefoot Books, we celebrate art and story that opens the hearts
and minds of children from all walks of life, focusing on themes that
encourage independence of spirit, enthusiasm for learning and respect
for the world's diversity. The welfare of our children is dependent on
the welfare of the planet, so we source paper from sustainably managed
forests and constantly strive to reduce our environmental impact.
Playful, beautiful and created to last a lifetime, our products combine
the best of the present with the best of the past to educate our
children as the caretakers of tomorrow.

www.barefootbooks.com

Josephine Evetts~Secker

studied at the University of London and the Jung Institute. She developed a Jungian practice in Canada while teaching English literature at the University of Calgary. She now practices in Yorkshire. She has lectured widely and published poetry, articles and book chapters. She has also written *The Barefoot Book of Mother and Daughter Tales*.

Helen Cann

is an illustrator and artist who paints in a shared studio in sunny Brighton. She regularly exhibits and also manages arts events. Before painting, she likes to immerse herself in researching the cultures she is depicting. Helen has illustrated many Barefoot Books favorites including *The Barefoot Book of Mother and Daughter Tales* and the Inuk Quartet.

Allan Corduner

trained at Bristol Old Vic and has a long association with the Royal Court Theatre as well as appearing at London's National Theatre. He performed in Carol Churchill's satire *Serious Money*, which transferred to Broadway. His film career includes Mike Leigh's *Vera Drake* and among his audio book credits are *The Book Thief* and Cornelia Funke's *Inkdeath*.